MR. MEN
Winter Sports

Roger Hargreaves

Original concept by
Roger Hargreaves

Written and illustrated by
Adam Hargreaves

EGMONT

Little Miss Somersault and Mr Snow had one big thing in common.

They loved snow.

They loved sledging.

They loved making snowballs.

And they loved making snowmen.

But most of all, Little Miss Somersault loved skiing.

So this year, Little Miss Somersault went on holiday to the mountains, where she could ski to her heart's content.

There were people who could ski very well, like Little Miss Somersault.

There were people who were beginners, like Little Miss Tiny.

And there were people who could not ski at all.

Like Mr Clumsy.

OUCH!

Skiing was not the only thing Mr Clumsy could not do.

He could not toboggan like Mr Snow.

OUCH!

He could not snowboard like Mr Busy.

OUCH!

He even had trouble drinking hot chocolate!

What a mess.

While she was in the mountains, Little Miss Somersault decided it would be fun to hold a competition.

She organised two events.

A ski jump trick event and a downhill race.

Mr Muddle wanted an uphill race, but everybody agreed that this was not such a good idea.

It was not surprising that in the ski jump Little Miss Somersault performed an amazing trick.

She flew through the air, somersaulting and twisting and pirouetting, with the grace of a swan.

Mr Snow, the judge of all things snowy, was very impressed.

Mr Snow was not so impressed with Mr Bump's trick.

Mr Bump had all the grace of a hippopotamus.

And Little Miss Dotty's trick was the wrong sort of trick.

But it was a most unexpected person who won with a most unusual trick.

Mr Clumsy realised too late that he was approaching the ski jump too fast.

He tried to slow down, but tripped and was catapulted high into the air.

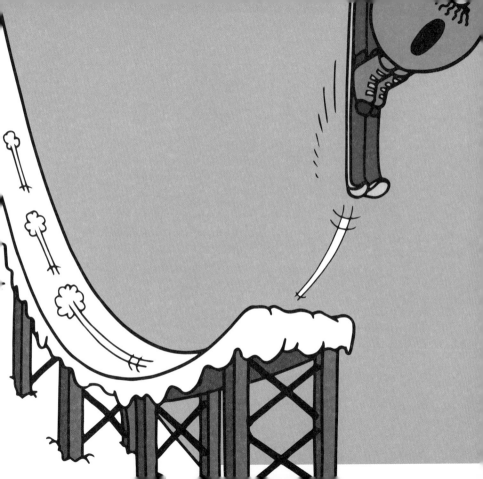

He twisted.

He turned.

He looped the loop.

And he barrel rolled through the air trying to get the right way up.

Mr Snow could not believe his eyes.

The crowd held its breath.

Mr Clumsy landed.

On one ski!

The crowd cheered and Mr Snow awarded first prize to Mr Clumsy.

It was then time for the downhill race.

Again, Little Miss Somersault was the favourite to win.

But, again, Mr Clumsy tripped.

And this time he rolled.

And rolled.

And rolled.

And the more he rolled the more snow he collected.

Until he was one giant snowball.

And as the snowball rolled faster and faster down the mountain the other racers were rolled up in it.

The snowball finally caught up with Little Miss Somersault just before the finishing line.

Where it rolled to a stop.

And Mr Clumsy won by a nose!

What an extraordinary feat of incompetence.

But Mr Clumsy had won both events.

Two cups in one day!

Which was two more cups than he had managed all week.

Cups of hot chocolate that is!